"Like the Sun, We will Live to Rise,
Like the Sun, We will Live & Die,
And then, Ignite Again."
                                        Chris Cornell

SILENT SUN

AYUSHMAN JAMWAL

Become
Shakespeare
.com

First published in 2018 by

Becomeshakespeare.com
Wordit Content Design & Editing Services Pvt. Ltd.
Unit - 26, Building A -1, NrWadala RTO,
Wadala (East), Mumbai 400037, India
T: +91 8080226699

Wordit Art Fund helps deserving authors publish their work by
providing monetary support. To apply for funding,
please visit us at
www.BecomeShakespeare.com

©
ISBN-978-93-88081-12-2

Disclaimers
This is a work of fiction. Names, characters, businesses,
places, events, locales, and incidents are either the products of
the author's imagination or used in a fictitious manner.
Any resemblance to actual persons, living or dead,
or actual events is purely coincidental.

Table of Contents

FOREWORD
Dr. Lalit Mangotra

When a good book is written, they say, humanity takes a step forward. The adage applies perfectly well to Ayushman Jamwal's anthology of poems, *Silent Sun*. The collection bespeaks mainly the virtues and flaws that make *Homo sapiens* human. If the twenty poems the book contains is a delineation of man's indomitable courage and intense energy; it also is a starkly honest and exceptionally sensitive evocation of man's imperfections, his unfulfilled desires, his frustration on failing to comprehend what he is, his fear of death and his obstinate efforts to forget the inviolable truth of death.

The poems project the persona of a man who leads a full and vibrant life. Two predominant emotions emerge from them. The first is of an unending quest for something that he cannot quite put a finger on. The reader wonders what he is looking for. Is it an ideal? If he has in mind such a one, the ideal is in fragments, scattered in time and space. The unrest of the mind drives him on and on, leaving him, as a consequence, an utter loner.

The second emotion is that of an emptiness which a sensitive man is bound to carry all his life. The void is inside him and he has to live with it. It creates in him a longing to find a partner to share his emptiness, but that longing more often than not remains unfulfilled. A quiescent longing does a tireless seeker make.

The powerful imagery which the poet has crafted to express his emotions is commendable. A master artist could not have done better to paint a rich array of feelings with his brush strokes. Word-pictures implanted into the matrix of each poem retain their sharpness in the reader's mind long after the poem is finished.

I need mention only a few of the poems to make my point. In *Omen*, the poet describes a mottled landscape cluttered with 'Shards of light and twisted shapes of human chaos' in which he comes face to face with Death, 'a scarred spectre at peace in the black.'

Unnerved, the poet confesses, 'All I can do is stare back.' In the chilling cold fear, he has a foreboding that neither faith nor love would stand 'her Godless gaze.'

Then take *Rama's Lament*. The poem brings out the discordance between the adulation of the devotees and what the protagonist feels about himself:

'They say I am a prophet of virtue and duty,

They cling to me for meaning, put me in gilded castles,
But I am hollow, just as that inanimate life…'

What sets this poem apart from the run-of-the-mill characterisation of Rama as a prosaic, principled and hard-hearted ruler who thought nothing of putting Sita through a fire-test and then sent her off to exile, is the godly hero's torment on having lost his beloved wife:

'I turned my back on her, and she returned to the earth,
Even death can't reunite us, my divinity is my curse…'

The poem enables us to see that, after all was said and done, a loving heart beat in Lord Rama's chest as well.

An inability to connect and communicate with someone emotionally and emphatically is what the poet regards as his greatest tragedy and pain. His quest is to meld with someone; and that quest is the main reason of his discontent. His loneliness is palpable. *I Think of You* and *Court Love and Fade Away* are two beautiful poems expressing this yearning. The first one is about the urge to look for a faceless soulmate, who embodies all that is beautiful and makes life worth living. It is a very delicate and exclusive feeling:

'A strange play of heart and mind,
Giving me what I can't hold or find,
Every smile, kiss & touch, I yearn for you,
Till then beloved,
I think of you.'

In the second poem, the poet, while conceding the mutability of love, affirms its divine fragrance which wafts for ages:

We may awaken to spurn each other,
We may turn some tragic pages,
Yet, the divinity of love is fleeting, is it not?
Like the Bard's tales, evergreen over the ages.

Bipolar Heart and *Nothing* are about the strange and incomprehensible ways of love, its magnetic web and the illogical manner in which one's own mind rebels against the self. One part of the mind feels the lover's racing heart, the abject surrender, hopes and dreams; yet, the other part is totally numb *(Nothing)*. In contrast, the narrator in *Bipolar Heart*, for all his scepticism, willingly gives in to the call of love.

Silent Sun is a tribute to the human spirit. While gods and nations have had their periods of rise and fall, man's spirit has held its own through the ages.

The poems comprising the anthology compel a reader to perceive life from a different perspective. There lies, to my mind, the success of the young poet.

Dr. Lalit Mangotra is a Sahitya Akademi award winning writer and poet. He serves as the President of the Dogri Sanstha in Jammu and Kashmir.

1

TEARS OF THE WANDERING MYSTIC

All I remember is the green of your eyes,
A storyteller's canvas of a limitless sky,
Memories of awe and wonder, now so distant,
I witnessed you perish, your zeal disappear,
I could not shed a tear.

I hold your words in my home,
The world calls it the greatest poem,
I yearn to find you between the lines,
As the verses dance in my mind,
I see a broken soul struggling to be kind.

You talk of family and love's eternal birds,
I see darkness and fear in your words,
Yet, an ungodly conviction tethered your heart,
You knew fate was fickle, but she felt like a boon,
You crumbled as she was taken too soon.

No faith in love, only its bane,

No bottle or smoke could end the pain,
Your children's devotion could not fill the hole,
Their love remains pure, but wasn't enough,
You weren't alone, you wallowed in your tragic
bluff.

Vigour in the pen, but the passion slowly faded,
No muse in the black, the thirst abandoned,
unsated,
You corralled new souls for a new start,
But a soulmate's spectre is too cruel a ploy,
You courted death when surrounded by joy.

Here I finish the tale of no hero, just a Man,
Journey of a delicate heart without a plan,
May you find peace in another life,
You may have seen love with a heretic's gaze,
I will have more faith in its grace.

I will have more faith in its grace.

2

I THINK OF YOU

Far away from savage civilisation,
In the sea of devotion and elevation,
Powerful stillness in the mist narcotic,
I douse my fury for purpose anew,
I think of you.

The concrete air is miles away,
I untie the knots, shed my skin again,
Stars engulf the sky with beautiful hues,
Haze consumes my memory's view,
I think of you.

I turn to the furious white waters,
Life-giving force like a deafening mortar,
I stand at the edge of this oblivion,
Tempted to see what lies through,
I think of you.

I walk on the fringes of the green sea,
The silent winter shroud advances fearlessly,
Warring realms united in a peaceful sliver,

I breathe in that alchemy under an endless blue,
I think of you.

In dark hills, I find a piece of moon,
On the stage, spirits ask about you,
No face, no frame, I say, and they're amused,
'Has hope driven you insane?', they ask,
'I know I will meet her someday', I laugh.

A strange play of heart and mind,
Giving me what I can't hold or find,
Every smile, kiss & touch, I yearn for you,
Till then beloved,
I think of you.

3

AM I NOT GOD'S CHILD?

For all the women facing and fighting the injustice of Triple Talaq

The union of two souls I thought,
Home for new life & love, I always sought,
Hoping for happiness, was I naïve?
He said it was God's decree, he could abandon
me & leave,
Discarded, a shroud of shame they wrap around
me.

Do you think the Prophet would grieve?

Is anger my right, or is it blasphemy?
I learned compassion from God, never savagery,
My child looks for his father,
He wipes my tears, wondering why I weep,
I teach him my faith, but fear what a man he
will be.

Do you think the Prophet would grieve?

How could he have such control over my life?
Why am I just a man's wife?
Where is my aspiration, my wings, my shield?
Was I raised to go to an alien home and yield?
I have been blind, my faith could not elevate
me.

Do you think the Prophet would grieve?

My justice is now in the hands of imposters,
Long beards, meagre hearts & no less than
monsters,
They twist God's intentions, make the faithful
cower,
I didn't even open the divine book, I gave them
this power,
Greed, misogyny and apathy, wrapped in holy
tapestry.

Do you think the Prophet would grieve?

There is no real sanctuary for me,
There is a roof, but no home to live free,
Faith wielded by the unkind, my apathy too is my
bane,

Others may hope, but I will just be another
name,
No salvation from the God I love, I decay
painfully.

Do you think the Prophet would grieve?

@Rajbir

4

RAIN

Kill me now, or this heat will do it painfully,
As if these knots of humanity weren't enough,
Steel webs and pointless chaos,
These insects scurry as the breeze turns rough.

Blind fury from a dark sky,
But a blessing of life and colour,
Ungrateful beasts seek shelter from this divinity,
I alone embrace this realm, I become its emperor.

The Heavens weep and rejoice,
The Earth is consumed by ecstasy,
Do mere mortals have a choice,
When fate beckons us to break free?

I yearn to fly into the roaring dark,
See the might of heaven on an endless canvas,
Breathe in some unearthly air,
Witness Deities and Monsters of another universe.
Purify this concrete heap,
Awaken these timid hearts,

Drag our souls up through this sweet fury,
A supernova's symphony for a brand new start.
The crucible of creation across the sky,
And here I am rooted to this domesticated hole,
I pound my chest to break my shell,
I court death, even for the hope of something
more.

The rain turns to a trickle as the gates close,
The stench and heat bury their claws,
I stare as heaven drifts away,
Leaving a static world of ugly flaws.

The sky is still, bright and boring,
The wagging of banal tongues is unnerving,
No hallowed phantoms, just doubt in my mind,
I wait for the Gods to be kind.

I wait for the Gods to be kind.

—◦◦◦—

5

OMEN

There is a dark space beyond my window,
Shards of light and twisted shapes of human
chaos,
She stands in the middle, as creatures wail in
despair,
Staring at me, a scarred spectre at peace in the
black,
All I can do is stare back.

Every night she appears, this unholy omen,
Making the air and inanimate restless,
The night is frozen, yet my skin burns,
She sniffs out my fear, drawing closer to me,
All I can do is stare back.

She floats with poise above me,
Her empty gaze piercing my heart,
I close my eyes seeking the shelter of conviction,
I find only empty words, an elusive peace,
All I can do is stare back.

I saw faith and love as cherished armour,
Still, she heralds a crippling futility,
No heavenly light at the edge, only chains of
solitude,
Fixated by her horrible truth, her Godless gaze,
All I can do is stare back.

Fear loosens its grip, a strange comfort breaks
my fever,
Am I broken for having accepted her truth?
My mortality comforts my yearning soul,
In her gaze, I find a fearful sanctuary,
All I can do is stare back.

What holds the hearts of priests and romantics?
Why does she show me my reflection every night,
As she slowly fades into the night once again,
She leaves me stunned with a tragic calmness,
And all I can do is stare back.

6

BIPOLAR HEART

Her passion is pure, divine and dangerous,
A fragile heart so fierce,
Black magic & whispers narcotic,
Fearlessness of a spirit so careless.

Her darkness is a terrible thing,
A disdain, daunting and crippling,
Indifference of a feverish trauma,
The taste of ash, no idle drama.

Her hurt is a sorrowful sight,
An invisible and heavy blight,
She only yearns to return to a better place,
Am I foolish to offer an embrace?

She decides to live behind a glass wall,
I look ahead, life moves on after all,
The phone rings, her name I don't imagine,
She speaks to me like nothing's happened.

She offers no haven, yet I want to fall,
Drown in the bright and black, the price is
small,
Life renewed again and again, like from above,
Is this healthy, or is this love?

7

MY BROKEN ANGEL

In the din and endless motion,
Her eyes liberate all the shadows,
A flair of grace and a warm glow,
And a painful sight of crippling sorrow,
A dark space so vast in a gentle soul.

She resonates light to the weary and lost,
Charity of joy in a time of bartered hearts,
Her skin is soft and delicate, with scars old and
new,
Wounds which fade beneath her alluring gaze,
The hurt deep within, showing no mercy.

She plays my heart strings, my broken angel,
I, a Man, yet a base creature, mute and
powerless,
A sigh & silence as she weeps behind a tired
smile,
I yearn an embrace to comfort her,
She crumbles in my arms, my love undivine.

All I do is hold her hand,
A silent prayer to draw out her grief,
Cruel fate dragging us to a forked road,
A struggle unforgiving,
A faith strong, but not enough.

Piety is for fools, and I am one today,
Hope for another plane, a world somewhere,
Where my angel blossoms with love enduring,
Where our brimming eyes can melt God's icy
heart,
There, under kinder stars, I will find you again.

8

THE LOST ARTIST

I show who I am on an empty page,
More truth in my hands, than what I say,
A cry for mercy in these words you recite,
Can you help me find the light?

Under the weight of my memory,
These words echo with all my fury,
Yet, alone and silent I tremble tonight,
Can you help me find the light?

In temples and churches, God seems so far,
No holy communion even at the bar,
I am fire by day, I am tears at night,
Can you help me find the light?

If only I could split my chest,
My heart could make so much sense,
I still toil to transcend your sight,
Can you help me find the light?

The soul in my veins gives me no peace,
My loathing and love will never cease,
Can you spare some compassion for what I
write?
Can you help me find the light?

9

NEON CHAOS

Harsh lights, harsh sounds, mangled concrete
veins,
The stench of greed, lust, gluttony and disdain,
On its fringes there are pitiful gambles and loss,
I am drawn to the heart of the Neon Chaos.

Conformed empty souls masquerade on its
edge,
In that perfumed crowd, I tiptoe on the ledge,
I just yearn to fall and hope to fly across,
Rest the darkest part of me in the Neon Chaos.

What the fuck is normal with unrest within?
Under these crumbling banners, I shed my skin,
No bells, no spires, no dogma, a nameless ethos,
No love, only hunger in this Neon Chaos.

The addict, the rich, the priest united in this
temple,
Wanderers, murderers and pretenders all
resemble,

Scarred and restless spirits, no figures of pathos,
The world feigns, they live free in the Neon
Chaos.

No King, Master or Crusader can make it depart,
Eternal sanctuary when God doesn't have a
heart,
In the Devil's palace, fate remains a coin toss,
In the hurt, ecstasy & freedom of the Neon
Chaos.

10

CONQUEROR IN A PRETTY DRESS

Don't let my smile deceive you,
I know who I am, I know what I can do,
Behold vast wings, just beyond my hair's caress,
You wonder why you're confused, let me confess,
I am a conqueror, and I wear a pretty dress.

Boiling blood of beasts, the appetite of savages,
Eyes lining my skin, I hear the rattling of cages,
Yet, I drink to my freedom, I savour my bliss,
I am ready, they will fear my fearlessness,
I am a conqueror, and I wear a pretty dress.

My love undefined, my taste unrefined,
My gaze undemure, my yearning perilously pure,
No contrived clocks, no fate under duress,
In bed or battlefield, I seek only my heart's excess,
I am a conqueror, and I wear a pretty dress.

No idle faith in my fragile veins,
Strength and beauty are mine, not my bane,
Even as I bleed, I don't walk on my knees,
I only forge empires above their simple heads,
I am a conqueror, and I wear a pretty dress.

Scarred and reborn every day,
Silent, powerful by my will, my way,
A spirit branded alien, but no more than human,
As I transcend your mind, you only witness,
I am a conqueror, and I wear a pretty dress.

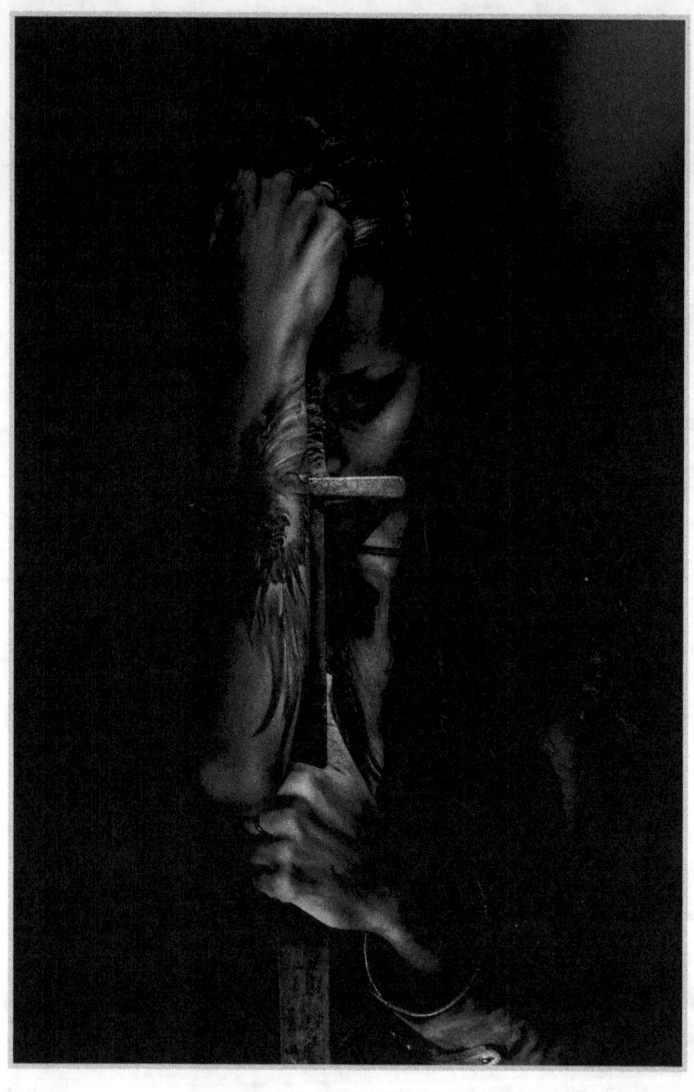

11
THE WARRIOR'S WIFE

He stumbles through the trees smearing them red,
His sword still burns with screams of dread,
The faint light of his lake house is all he sees,
To purge his demon from the battlefields.

At the end of his crimson road,
A breath away from his abode,
Peace eludes him like a crippling infection,
Only ash and spectres in his vision.

Above the lake, under an ungodly moon,
Phantoms of comrades & enemies marooned,
The bannerless dead tear him asunder,
They say, 'Come join us Brother'.

Into the water, he prepares to be free,
Scorpions in his mind showing no mercy,
The blade pressed to his heart, he doesn't ask why,
'I am a soldier', he says, 'I am meant to die'.

Two soft arms emerge and coil around him,
A heavenly warmth seeps into the darkness within,
He gazes into two bright eyes brimming with life,
He thinks, 'This farishta looks just like my wife.'

She clung to him as he reeked of death,
His beating heart was all she felt,
An obsessive devotion to bring him back,
Even the circling reaper feared her wrath.

A gentle touch of her lips is all she tried,
His spirit was reborn and the devil cried,
He drifted away in her embrace, a love so zealous,
The undead just wept, bitter and jealous.

No more doubt, no more pain,
He drank the life she offered from her gentle
frame,
Locked in each other, a passionate baptism in
the spray,
She gave him the only reason to live another day.

Two souls walk back healed,
He put down his flag, his thirsty steel,
He held her hand, faith renewed and fear
undone.
What is honour before the love of a woman.

@Rajbir

12

TRAGIC BEAUTY

A sea of memory with a dark muse,
Juvenile joy, yet sacred love anew,
Delicate warmth of a violent heart,
Nurturing malevolence in the dark,
Poisoned happiness primed in her arsenal,
It's so tragic, it's beautiful.

I paint a canvas with my fire,
Wielding my precarious desire,
My dark muse scorns with enchanting fury,
She torches my art, deems it unsavoury,
Covered in ash, my smile is blissful,
It's so tragic, it's beautiful.

Fleeting hope is all she has given,
Yet, life is sweet an edge from oblivion,
No tradition or equation for the soul,
In her shadow there's decay, but I am whole,
So many scars, but I'm not delusional,
It's so tragic, it's beautiful.

She is not love, just a fascinating thing,
A human tempest held by glass strings,
Night and day, rising and falling together,
Love and disdain in one ungodly spectre,
Blossoming and withering, I witness her,
unmerciful,
It's so tragic, it's beautiful.

13

SILENT SUN

A power so great in a shell so frail,
Celestial decree from the primordial well,
Wading through the past with an eye on eternity,
Defiant, even on the edge of oblivion,

I am the Silent Sun.

Sleepless under the gaze of my fables,
The empire of my zeal, strong yet unstable,
I seek no dominion over things, only destiny,
I fear a life of static peace, unremembered,
undone,

I am the Silent Sun.

I am no empty wanderer, abject and meek,
In crusades and solitude, only meaning I seek,
Gods and nations, I am tethered to all,
They are preys of time only I outrun,

I am the Silent Sun.

All the pain I have ever known,
Every joy, love and faith reborn,
All intertwined in my fragile veins,
Beyond memory, this enlightened chaos will
burn,

I am the Silent Sun.

No king, No slave, No hero, No prophet,
I am that fire that is and then no more,
Chains and wings of my choice,
A will no less or greater than human,

I am the Silent Sun.

14
RAMA'S LAMENT

They chant my name, with fiery hearts they scream,
They call me a saviour, from a wise mystic's dream,
I buried their villain, washed the earth's soul clean,
I just smile at them with a heavy heart,

For I miss my beloved queen.

They marvel at me and call me divine decree,
They say I am a prophet of virtue and duty,
They cling to me for meaning, put me in gilded
castles,
But I am hollow, just as that inanimate life,

For I miss my beloved wife.

I was only Godly with her by my side,
I was only a King when I felt her strength nearby,
I was only a Man when her hand was in mine,
Only for her did I make the heavens kneel,

Oh, how I miss my beloved queen.

My father always told me to follow my heart,
Why did my earthly duty tear it apart?
I sit atop a golden tower as my people hope and
pray,
I breathe in these clouds, but they taste so damn
stale,

Oh, how I miss my beloved wife.

Rebirth, this power may be mine,
How do I redeem myself? No other can play her part,
I once roamed the earth as Narsimha, a
grotesque beast,
He protected his child, he had more of a heart,

Oh, how I miss my beloved queen.

I turned my back on her, and she returned to the
earth,
Even death can't reunite us, my divinity is my curse,
I see her in all creation, in the compassion of our sons,
They'll be better men, as her love mocks me the same,
Let humanity see, even a God hangs his head in
shame.

Oh, how I miss my beloved wife.

15

WE REMEMBER, OUR NATION FORGETS

For the Kashmiri Pandits, refugees in their own country

We still see the fire, we still see the fury,
Memories of men turning to demons so clearly,
Bonds of ash as chaos consumed our beloved
Valley,
Driven out like animals, a purge without regret,
We remember, our nation forgets.

We still see our slaughtered children at night,
We still hear wailing women, and monsters in
delight,
Homes torn down as our claim was less holy,
Legacies wiped out with one stroke of hate,
We remember, our nation forgets.

They rise against injustice with tempests untamed,
In one voice they shout #NotInMyName,

We're absent from their hearts, their rage has a
faith,
Scowling at the saffron of our forebears with no
lament,
We remember, our nation forgets.

Away from our home, but the Tricolour is in our
hearts,
We pick up books, we salute, we toil for a new
start,
Voiceless we march and fight our cruel destiny,
We try so hard, but the nightmare refuses to relent,
We remember, our nation forgets.

Our tragedy has no God, we are branded
heathens,
We may be Hindus and Pandits, but are we not
Indians?
Refugees in our country, an identity close to
extinction,
No promised land, we built a home with blood &
sweat,
We remember, our nation forgets.

We remember, our nation forgets.

16

NOTHING

She loves me with so much fire,
She loves me with a powerful desire,
Her passion is such a daunting thing,
A blaze of light so enduring,

I, feel nothing.

I feel her racing heart behind her bliss,
I feel her lost in our gentle kiss,
I fear that hope in those eyes brimming,
I lay beside her as she holds me sweetly
dreaming,

I, feel nothing.

She weaves the future before our eyes,
She seeks blessings from the endless sky,
I smile, yet no more than a lie,
Elusive tears as my reflection takes a beating,

I, feel nothing.

Her love and devotion was so rare,
The dark truth was so easy to bare,
Nothing to offer, she just wanted me to hold her,
Even in her embrace, I yearned for something,

I, felt nothing.

A slow decay she didn't deserve,
Only fury and remorse did my confession earn,
Scorched yet cold they say is the feeling,
Yet, even in the desolation of everything,

I, feel nothing.

Her love is too strong for life to be unkind,
A kindred soul soon found her, as I remained
blind,
Empty in light and dark, am I such a cursed
thing?
I seek that divine spark, even an ungodly
reckoning,

Yet I fear, I will feel nothing.

17

THE GLASS WALL

I see all of you just a breath away,
No lifeless sand in my veins today,
Only a glimpse of sanctuary before nightfall,
I kneel defeated before this Glass Wall.

I may drift blissfully under your eyes,
So close, yet a stranger with no goodbyes,
A faith in destiny just to seem tall,
As I feel eternity in every inch of this Glass Wall.

A gentle heart & words are all I am,
Human clay that can barely withstand,
Compassion, only in what I recall,
I decay patiently behind this Glass Wall.

My wings tremble with regret,
I bury the will to fly away and forget,
The virtue of hope only makes me small,
I stare at all of my fear in this Glass Wall.

Time to shed this visage for a new start,
There's dwindling inspiration in coming apart,
I grow weary of your smile at this masquerade
ball,
Yet, I still wonder,

Can I walk away from this Glass Wall?

18

COURT LOVE AND FADE AWAY

Look at me and sever your ties,
Let the fear melt away before your eyes,
Sleep lies far away from you and me,
Daunting choices loom above, eager to pass by.

Shed the burden of every consequence,
Ease the restless doubt in your gaze,
Your hands tremble, yet your heart yearns,
Find sanctuary in my embrace.

Why did we steal ourselves away from the world?
Why did we root ourselves in this solitary place?
I heard your wordless beckon, coy yet electric,
Drown with me in what you have already accepted.

Everything about this moment stirs your soul to
burn,
Why cower before a future that remains uncertain?
Just look at me, and I at you,
Free, yet bound to the touch, rush and glow.

We may awaken to spurn each other,
We may turn some tragic pages,
Yet, the divinity of love is fleeting, is it not?
Like the Bard's tales, evergreen over the ages.

My words ring true from my doomed heart,
Let's Court,
Let's Love,
Let's Fade Away.

19
THE CURSED ROCKSTAR

My words are heavy,
My truth, I struggle to carry,
Memories like a stifling collar,
Before this daunting dark, I only grow smaller,
I dive into this crowd with just my voice,
I cry, they rejoice.

They chant my name with all their heart,
My walls tremble, I almost fall apart,
I yearn for silence, a small piece of sun,
Even there darkness creeps, my mind comes
undone,
I run back to the hungry masses with very little
choice,
I cry, they rejoice.

They call my words an eternal sermon,
Dark and vivid shards of a life uncertain,
They wade into my sorrow tethered to their light,

They marvel at me consumed in this blight,
The fame of futile enlightenment, yet a life
devoid,
I cry, they rejoice.

My spirit grows weary with every song,
The exorcism of my music is not too strong,
No wisdom or melody to kill my monsters,
Endless love and devotion, but no faith to
conjure,
I shed every breath now, into the night I fly,

Now I rejoice, they cry.

20

MAY THE VALLEY HEAR ME ROAR

For the brave patriots defending Kashmir

I am armed, I am ready,
I am guided by my duty,
No masks to hide who I am,
I tear through the smoke and chaos,
I challenge you to test my mettle,

Hear me BOY, I am IMMORTAL

You scamper and hide in these dark alleys,
To ash you turn my beautiful Valley,
You strike from the sanctuary of crowds,
False prophets and death dealers in your head,
I may fall beneath the stones you hurl,

Hear me BOY, I am IMMORTAL

I am a soldier of the Tricolour,
I walk proudly wrapped in the banner,
I am bound to this land same as you,
But I am ready to die protecting, even the likes
of you,
Under your blows, I will not buckle,

Hear me BOY, I am IMMORTAL

Call your crusade whatever you like,
Follow which ever Devil you may find,
You are an abated captive of a poisonous
thought,
And you didn't even put up a fight.
I am here to protect what is ours, but I will not settle,

Hear me BOY, I am IMMORTAL

If my words fail, if fury still blurs your vision,
Meet me face to face on an open field,
Let us test our conviction.
I am the will of a billion hearts,
And when the dust settles after our brief battle,
I shall tower above you, and you shall see BOY,

I AM IMMORTAL

About the Author

Ayushman Jamwal is a Senior News Editor at CNN-News18. He completed his graduation and post-graduation in Britain at the prestigious Cardiff University School of Journalism, and was inducted into the University's Honour Roll.

He started writing poetry when he was a student at the Doon School in Dehradun. His first poetry collection 'Chameleon Lights' was featured in the top 10 poetry bestseller list 2017 on Amazon.com.

Ayushman also serves as a Board member of the KunwarViyogi Memorial Trust, established to promote and preserve the Dogri language spoken by the Duggar community of the Shivalik foothills. He curates the 'Cultural Cocktail: Youth For Art' initiative, a platform for innovation with a focus on convergence of classical, contemporary, regional and global literature and art forms.

He lives with his parents, younger brother, grandmother and dog Leo.